# where did that

*for all the Earth babies –*
*every one a star*
*D.G.*

WHERE DID THAT BABY COME FROM?
A DOUBLEDAY BOOK 0 385 60619 2

Published in Great Britain by Doubleday,
an imprint of Random House Children's Books

This edition published 2004

1 3 5 7 9 10 8 6 4 2

Copyright © Debi Gliori, 2004
Designed by Ian Butterworth

RANDOM HOUSE CHILDREN'S BOOKS
61–63 Uxbridge Rd, London W5 5SA
A division of The Random House Group Ltd

RANDOM HOUSE AUSTRALIA (PTY) LTD
20 Alfred Street, Milsons Point, Sydney,
New South Wales 2061, Australia

RANDOM HOUSE NEW ZEALAND LTD
18 Poland Road, Glenfield, Auckland 10, New Zealand

RANDOM HOUSE (PTY) LTD
Endulini, 5A Jubilee Road, Parktown 2193, South Africa

THE RANDOM HOUSE GROUP Limited Reg. No. 954009
www.kidsatrandomhouse.co.uk

A CIP catalogue record for this book is available from the British Library.

Printed and bound in Singapore

# baby come from ?

### Debi Gliori

Doubleday

Where did that baby come from,
and can we take it back?
It wails and squeaks, its nappy leaks —
it's an insomniac.

Where did that baby come from,
did it float down from the sky?
It's got no wings or feathered things —
I don't think it can fly.

Where did that baby come from,
did it grow out of a seed?
Will roses grow between its toes
or is it just a weed?

Where did that baby come from,
did you buy it in a store?
Amongst the lots of bargain tots —
please don't buy any more.

SPECI
OFFER
free ~ range
babies

**W**here did that baby come from,
did you find it at the zoo?
You didn't heed the 'Please don't feed'
but brought it home with you.

Where did that baby come from,
did you build it from a kit?
All it can do is pee and poo —
Does it have a missing bit?

Where did that baby come from,
did you bake it like a bun?
Yeuchh - take a look - it's not quite cooked —
don't make another one.

Where did that baby come from,
did you fish it out the sea?
It doesn't swim, it has no fins —
come on, let's set it free.

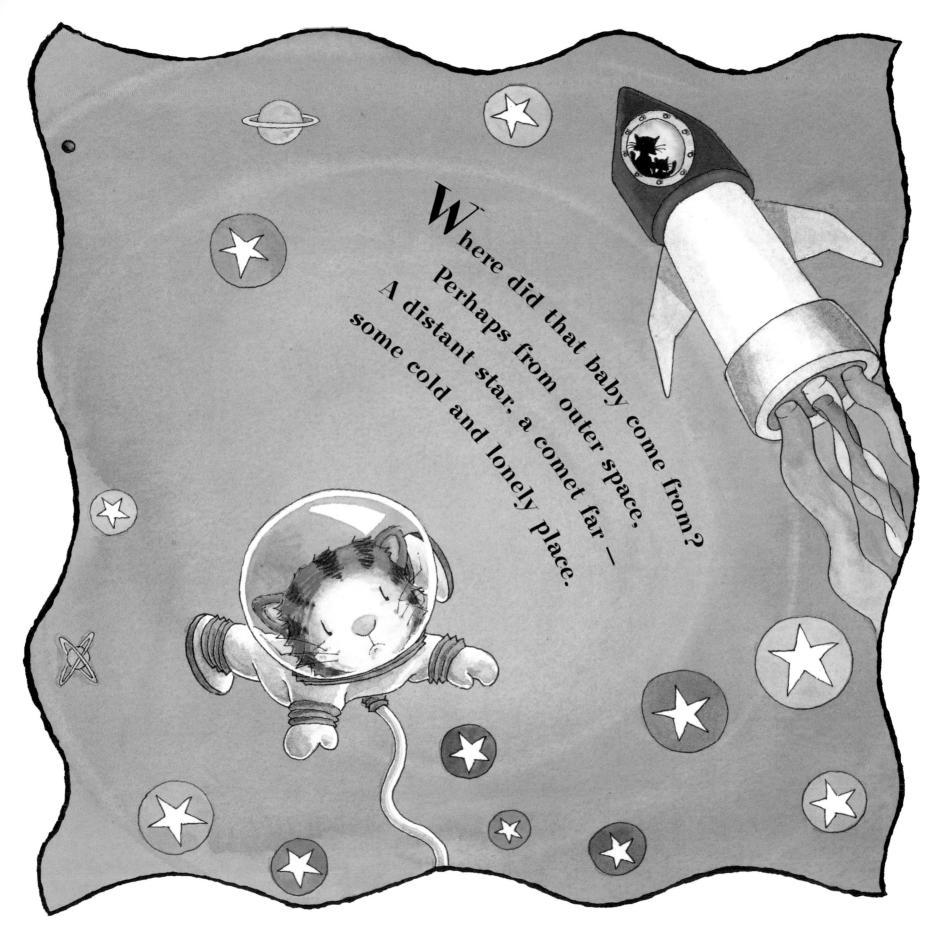

Where did that baby come from?
Perhaps from outer space,
A distant star, a comet far —
some cold and lonely place.

Why is that baby crying?
Oh, baby, why d'you weep?
I'll keep you warm and safe from harm
and help you fall asleep.

Baby, why are you laughing?
Was it something that I said?
A peek-a-boo, or I-love-you,
a kiss dropped on your head?

I think our baby comes from
the place I come from too.

Our place of birth was planet Earth,
this baby, me ... and you.

# CONTENTS

In this book we are introduced to the Maynard family. We will meet Mr
and Mrs Maynard, their children Tom and Emma, and Tom and Emma's
grandparents John and Margaret. Compare how they enjoy themselves with
other families having fun fifty years ago.

# CIRCUS

## These acrobats are performing in front of the audience.

All the acts in this circus are performed by people. There are jugglers, tightrope walkers, clowns, acrobats and trapeze artists. The performers travel all around the world.

# FIFTY YEARS AGO
# Having Fun

Karen Bryant-Mole

WAYLAND

## Titles in the series
### At Home
### Going on a Trip
### Having Fun
### In the High Street

Find Wayland on the Internet at http://www.wayland.co.uk

**All Wayland books encourage children to read and help them improve their literacy.**

✓ The contents page, page numbers, headings and index help locate specific pieces of information.

✓ The glossary reinforces alphabetic knowledge and extends vocabulary.

✓ The further information section suggests other books dealing with the same subject.

✓ Find out more about how this book is specifically relevant to the National Literacy Strategy on page 31.

Editor: Carron Brown
Consultant: Norah Granger
Cover design: White Design
Inside design: Michael Leaman
Production controller: Carol Titchener

First published in 1998 by
Wayland Publishers Limited,
61 Western Road, Hove,
East Sussex BN3 1JD

Typeset in England by
Michael Leaman Design Partnership
Printed and bound in Italy by L.G. Canale &
C.S.p.A Turin

British Library in Cataloguing Data
Bryant-Mole, Karen
     Having Fun. – (Fifty years ago)
     1. Family recreation – Great Britain – History
     – 20th century – Juvenile literature
     2. Great Britain – Social conditions – 1945
     – Juvenile literature
     3. Great Britain – Social life and customs –
     1945 – Juvenile literature
     I. Title 941'. 085

ISBN 0 7502 2264 6

Picture acknowledgements
The publishers would like to thank the following
for allowing their pictures to be used in this book:
Corbis UK cover; Getty Images 5, 9, 11, 15, 19, 23,
25; Topham Picturepoint 7, 13, 17, 21; Wayland
Picture Library/ Stuart Weir  cover [inset], 6, 8,
10, 12, 14, 16, 20, 22, 24.

## These performers and their elephants practised their act before the show.

A long time ago, most circuses had performing animals. As well as elephants, there were often sea lions, bears, tigers and lions. Many people today think it is wrong to see wild animals perform tricks.

## I remember...

Margaret Maynard is Tom and Emma's grandmother. She remembers how excited all the children were when the circus came to town. 'A few days before the circus arrived, posters advertising the circus were stuck up. Then the huge circus tent went up. The animals lived in cages. I remember the smell from the cages being really strong.

# The Maynard family are going to Portugal for a holiday.

Portugal is thousands of kilometres away from the Maynards' home. The Maynards are flying to Portugal by plane. They will stay in a hotel near the beach. Mr and Mrs Maynard are looking forward to the hot, sunny weather. Tom and Emma can't wait to go to the children's club.

# These children had their holiday in England.

Fifty years ago, most people did not go abroad for their holidays. Instead, a lot of people went to the seaside. Donkey rides along the beach were very popular.

## I remember...

John Maynard is Tom and Emma's grandfather. When he was a boy, he used to stay in a seaside guest house. 'One year, it did nothing but rain all week. We had to leave the guest house after breakfast and couldn't come back until tea-time. It was too cold and wet to go on the beach, so I spent most of the week playing the slot machines in the penny arcade.'

# Tom is having a birthday party at a sports centre.

Tom decided to have his birthday party here because he and his friends really enjoy sport. There are lots of activities for the children. Tom's mum and dad bring party food for the children to eat afterwards.

# This girl had her birthday party at home.

Fifty years ago, most children had their birthday parties at home. They usually played party games such as Blind Man's Buff, Hunt the Thimble and O'Grady Says.

## I remember...

John enjoyed birthday parties but he didn't enjoy getting ready for them. 'My mum used to make me wear my best clothes. She scrubbed my face clean and brushed my hair so hard I thought it would fall out. Then she put some of dad's hair cream on my hair to make it shiny and keep it flat.'

## Emma enjoys playing in adventure playgrounds.

Emma likes pretending that this wobbly bridge is in the jungle. She pretends that if she falls off, she might get eaten by crocodiles. If she really fell off, she wouldn't get hurt because there is a soft surface underneath the bridge.

# This child liked to play on the swings.

Most playgrounds were covered in concrete. If a child fell off the swing he or she could have been badly hurt. Today, safety is very important.

## I remember...

Margaret liked to play on the slide when she went to the playground. 'I liked the slide because it was scary and exciting at the same time. It felt so high up and it was such a long way to the ground. Once, I went so fast I shot right off the end.'

# DANCING

## Emma and Tom enjoy going to a disco at their school.

Discos are fun. You can dance with a big group of friends or with one friend. You can even dance by yourself. The music is very loud. It is usually quite dark with flashing lights.

# These children learned to do ballroom dancing.

When grown-ups went to dances fifty years ago, they usually did ballroom dancing. They did special dances like the waltz and the foxtrot. Each dance had its own steps and music. You danced with a partner.

## I remember...

John hated ballroom dancing when he was a boy. 'Every Saturday morning I had to go to ballroom dancing lessons. I was useless. My partner was a girl called Gwen. I was always standing on her feet.'

# SWIMMING

## Tom is sliding down the slide at the swimming pool.

The Maynard family all go swimming on Friday evenings. Emma likes the wave machine. After they have been swimming they have a hot shower. Then they have a drink and some crisps at the swimming pool cafe.

# FIFTY YEARS AGO

## The girls in this picture had swimming lessons.

Fifty years ago, swimming pools were usually called swimming baths. There were no slides or wave machines. The buildings were not warm and it felt chilly when you got out of the water.

## I remember...

Margaret learned to swim when she was eight years old. 'I had a really strict teacher called Mrs Hunt. We were so scared of her that we did exactly what we were told. When she said swim, we swam.'

## The Maynards are enjoying a ride at a theme park.

Tom's favourite ride at the park is the big dipper. It makes his stomach feel funny as he goes up and down. Sophie likes the ride in a boat. It hurtles down a hill and splashes through some water.

# These children liked to ride on the merry-go-round.

This ride was part of a travelling fair that went to different towns and villages. As well as rides there would have been side-shows, such as hoop-la, and fortune-tellers. Today, fairground rides are faster and more exciting.

## I remember...

John remembers when the fair came to his town. 'We couldn't wait for school to end when the fair was in town. My friend, Jack, had his fortune told one year. The fortune teller said he would get married and have three children. We all laughed but twenty years later, Jack had a wife and three kids.'

# BONFIRE NIGHT

## These people are watching a fireworks display.

The Maynards always go to a big firework display on Bonfire Night. Everybody must buy a ticket to get in. This money is spent on fantastic fireworks. The Maynards like going to a display because it is safe and well organised.

# FIFTY YEARS AGO

## This girl lit the fireworks in her back garden.

In the past, many people were badly burned by fireworks. Today, there is a firework code that tells people how to use fireworks safely. Children should never be allowed to light fireworks.

### I remember...

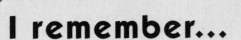

Margaret remembers one bonfire party she went to. 'We were eating toffee apples and having a lovely time. Then some of the boys lit some fireworks called Jumping Jacks. They were firecrackers that jumped all around the place. One of them jumped into my brother's boot by accident. I'd never heard anyone scream so loud. He's still got the scars from the burns.'

# Tom and Emma love playing computer games.

Tom and Emma have lots of toys. They like playing with construction sets to build moving machines. They also have an electric car racing set.

# This little girl liked playing with her toy doll.

Fifty years ago, children had fewer toys than they do now. But, just as today, toys were often like the things that children saw around them. Doll's prams were just like real prams. Toy trains looked like actual steam trains.

## I remember...

Margaret had a toy tea-set. 'My tea set was made out of china. It had pink roses on it, just like the real tea set my mum and dad had. I used to have pretend tea parties with my doll who was called Heather and my teddy who was called Albert.'

## Emma enjoys doing judo.

Emma goes to a judo club every week. She enjoys judo because it is fun and it keeps her fit. It might look rough but the idea is to get the opponent on the mat without hurting him or her.

# Boxing used to be a popular sport for boys.

Not many boys do boxing as a sport today. Boxers often get punched in the head. They can get badly injured. Today, many boxers wear head guards to protect them.

## I remember...

John used to like playing sport. 'I was really sporty. Hockey, football, cricket – you name it, I did it. I never did boxing. A lot of people thought it was a good sport for boys. They thought it kept them out of trouble and used up their energy.

## The Maynards are going to the cinema to watch a film together.

There are lots of different screens at this cinema, so there is usually a film that all the family will like. Before they sit down, they usually buy some drinks and a big box of popcorn.

## These children used to watch films by themselves.

On Saturday mornings, many cinemas had special children's shows. The children were brought to the cinema by their parents and left there to enjoy the films.

### I remember...

Margaret used to go to the cinema every Saturday morning. 'Every week there was a film, a cartoon and a serial that carried on from one week to the next. We really enjoyed it. It was very noisy. We all cheered the goodies and booed the baddies.'

# GLOSSARY

 **big dipper** A fairground ride, with train-type carriages that run on tracks.

 **hoop-la** A fairground game where hoops are thrown over prizes. If the hoop lands around the prize, you win it.

 **circus tent** The huge tent where the circus is performed, sometimes called a big top.

 **merry-go-round** A fairground ride, sometimes also called a roundabout or a carousel.

 **doll's pram** This doll's pram looks like real prams did fifty years ago.

 **steam train** This toy steam train looks like the real trains of fifty years ago.

 **guest house** A small hotel where bed, breakfast and an evening meal are provided.

 **toffee apple** An apple on a stick, coated in hot toffee that has been left to cool.

 **hair cream** A sort of lotion that is combed through the hair to make it shiny.

 **trapeze artist** Someone who does circus tricks hanging from swinging bars, high up in the circus tent.

# FURTHER INFORMATION

*People Having Fun* by K. Bryant-Mole
  (People through History series - Wayland, 1996)

*Toys* by K. Bryant-Mole (History from Objects series -
  Wayland, 1994)

*Toys discovered through History* (Linkers series -
  A & C Black, 1996)

*Seaside* by R. Thomson  (Changing Times - Watts, 1994)

*Toys and Games* by R. Thomson (Changing Times series -
  Watts, 1994)

*Having Fun in Grandma's Day* by F. Gardner
  (In Grandma's Day - Evans, 1997)

**Use this book for teaching literacy**

This book can help you in the literacy hour in the following ways:

✓ Children can extend the skills of reading non-fiction. There are two levels of text given, a simple version and a more advanced level.

✓ They can recognise that non-fiction books with similar themes can present similar information in different ways.

✓ They can be encouraged to ask their relatives about their lives when they were children and learn indirectly about history.

✓ They can imagine and write stories about how they would have had fun fifty years ago, for example.

# INDEX

# Garden

Katie Dicker

Published by Evans Brothers Limited
2A Portman Mansions
Chiltern Street
London W1U 6NR

© Evans Brothers Limited 2009

Produced for Evans Brothers Limited by
White-Thomson Publishing Ltd

Printed in China by New Era Printing Co. Ltd
Printed on chlorine-free paper from sustainably managed sources.

Educational consultant: Sue Palmer MEd FRSA FEA
Project manager: Katie Dicker
Picture research: Amy Sparks
Design: Balley Design Limited
Creative director: Simon Balley
Designer/Illustrator: Andrew Li

For Mia

British Library Cataloguing in Publication Data

Dicker, Katie
   Garden. - (Out and about) (Sparklers)
   1. Gardens - Juvenile literature
   I. Title
   635

ISBN: 978 0 2375 3877 4

# Contents

# Get gardening!

Come and help us water the garden.

sprinkle

4

What tools do YOU use

when you're gardening?

5

# Planting seeds

flower bed

In spring, we plant seeds in the ground.

This rake smoothes the soil and pulls up weeds.

7

# Time to grow

sweet smell

strawberry

What's happened to the plant you watered?

8

Some plants are grown in a greenhouse.

11

# Garden visitors

buzz!

Why are bees attracted to the flowers in summer?

13

# By the pond

What plants and animals live in a pond?

What other garden

creatures can you see?

sparkle!

17

# On the ground

lawnmower

keep straight!

What happens to the grass in summer?

18

In autumn, it's time to collect up the leaves.

sweep!

19

# Garden party!

Which friend will you catch next?

# Notes for adults

**Sparklers** books are designed to support and extend the learning of young children. The **Food We Eat** titles won a Practical Pre-School Silver Award and the **Body Moves** titles won a Practical Pre-School Gold Award. The books' high-interest subjects link in to the Early Years curriculum and beyond. Find out more about Early Years and reading with children from the National Literacy Trust (www.literacytrust.org.uk).

**Themed titles**
**Garden** is one of four **Out and About** titles that encourage children to explore outdoor spaces. The other titles are:
**Park          Seaside          Wood**

A CD to accompany the series (available from Evans Publishing Group tel 020 7487 0920 or email sales@evansbrothers.co.uk) provides sound effects from each environment, as well as popular songs and rhymes that relate to outdoor exploration.

**Areas of learning**
Each **Out and About** title helps to support the following Foundation Stage areas of learning:
*Personal, Social and Emotional Development*
*Communication, Language and Literacy*
*Mathematical Development*
*Knowledge and Understanding of the World*
*Physical Development*
*Creative Development*

**Making the most of reading time**
When reading with younger children, take time to explore the pictures together. Ask children to find, identify, count or describe different objects. Point out colours and textures. Allow quiet spaces in your reading so that children can ask questions or repeat your words. Try pausing mid-sentence so that children can predict the next word. This sort of participation develops early reading skills.

Follow the words with your finger as you read. The main text is in Infant Sassoon, a clear, friendly font designed for children learning to read and write. The labels and sound effects add fun and give the opportunity to distinguish between levels of communication. Where appropriate, labels, sound effects or main text may be presented phonically. Encourage children to imitate the sounds.

As you read the book, you can also take the opportunity to talk about the book itself with appropriate vocabulary such as "page", "cover", "back", "front", "photograph", "label" and "page number".

You can also extend children's learning by using the books as a springboard for discussion and further activities. There are a few suggestions on the facing page.

### Pages 4–5: Get gardening!
Give children a garden space of their own to dig the soil, water the plants and watch the garden grow. Children without a garden could make a miniature garden, a window box or a hanging basket. Explain to children what different garden tools are used for.

### Pages 6–7: Planting seeds
Encourage children to plant seeds of their own in indoor plant pots or outdoor spaces. Talk to children about the reasons why we aerate the soil and remove harmful weeds. Children may also enjoy acting out some gardening activities such as sowing seeds, digging flower beds and raking the soil.

### Pages 8–9: Time to grow
Help children to make their own growing grass. Put a handful of grass seeds into an old pair of tights, add sawdust and make a round 'head'. Draw a face with a marker pen. Water the top of the 'head' every day for a week until the grass 'hair' appears. Encourage children to cut the grass/hair with safety scissors when it gets too long. Children may also enjoy a sunflower growing competition.

### Pages 10–11: Vegetable patch
Draw pictures (or cut photographs from magazines) of common fruit and vegetables. Encourage children to group them into colours or order of size. Use the activity to talk about which vegetables are commonly grown in a garden and the importance of eating fruit and vegetables as part of a balanced diet. Children may also enjoy growing (or tending to) a simple indoor herb garden.

### Pages 12–13: Garden visitors
Explain to children why a garden is a popular place for animals to visit at different times of the year. Encourge children to record the birds that visit their garden. They could make a simple bird feeder or a bird-bath to entice their feathered friends. Children may also enjoy making a bird's nest from twigs.

### Pages 14–15: By the pond
Children may enjoy playing 'musical lily pads'. Cut out big water lilies from green paper and place them on the floor at varying intervals. Make sure there is one less lily pad than children playing. Ask children to walk or dance around the room and hop onto a lily pad when the music stops. The child without a lily pad leaves the game, and one pad is removed before the next go.

### Pages 16–17: Garden creatures
Encourage children to record the creatures they find amongst the grass, soil, flowers and leaves of a garden. Use books or the Internet to help children identify what the creatures are. Children may also enjoy making ladybird or butterfly wings from card and tissue paper. Children could wear the wings using simple elastic arm bands.

### Pages 18–19: On the ground
Encourage children to think about different ways they can help in the garden during the changing seasons. How does the garden change at different times of the year? In the spring, children may enjoy collecting rainwater that falls to the ground, to use in the garden in summer, for example.

### Pages 20–21: Garden party!
Help children to make their own tepee or A-shape tent with garden canes and an old sheet. Children may also enjoy party activities such as having an outdoor tea party, traditional games of hide and seek or decorating the bare trees of a garden in winter to create a party atmosphere.

# Index

**Picture acknowledgements:**
**Alamy:** 13 (Peter Arnold, Inc); **Corbis:** 7 (Ariel Skelley), 10 (Tom Stewart), 14 (Sandra Ivany/Brand X), 15 (Flirt), 20 (H. Benser/zefa); **Getty Images:** cover girl (altrendo images), 4 (Michael Hitoshi), 8 (Stockbyte), 9 (Windsor & Wiehahn), 11 (Birgid Allig), 16 (Tom Morrison), 18 (Pierre Bourrier), 21 (Ghislain & Marie David de Lossy); **IStockphoto:** cover sky (JLFCapture), 6 (Dan Rossini); **Photolibrary:** 19 (Leanne Temme); **Shutterstock:** cover garden (Filip Fuxa), cover pink flowers (Mandy Godbehear), 2–3 flowers (Stephen Aaron Rees), 5 watering can (Sz Akos), 5 spade and trowel (Sony Ho), 5 garden fork (Sony Ho), 5 trug (Rtimages), 12 (nikolpetr), 17 butterfly (Aron Brand), 17 ladybird (Yellowj), 17 mouse (kenxro), 17 spider (Arie v.d. Wolde), 22–23 flowers (Stephen Aaron Rees), 24 flowers (Stephen Aaron Rees).